The Haunted House

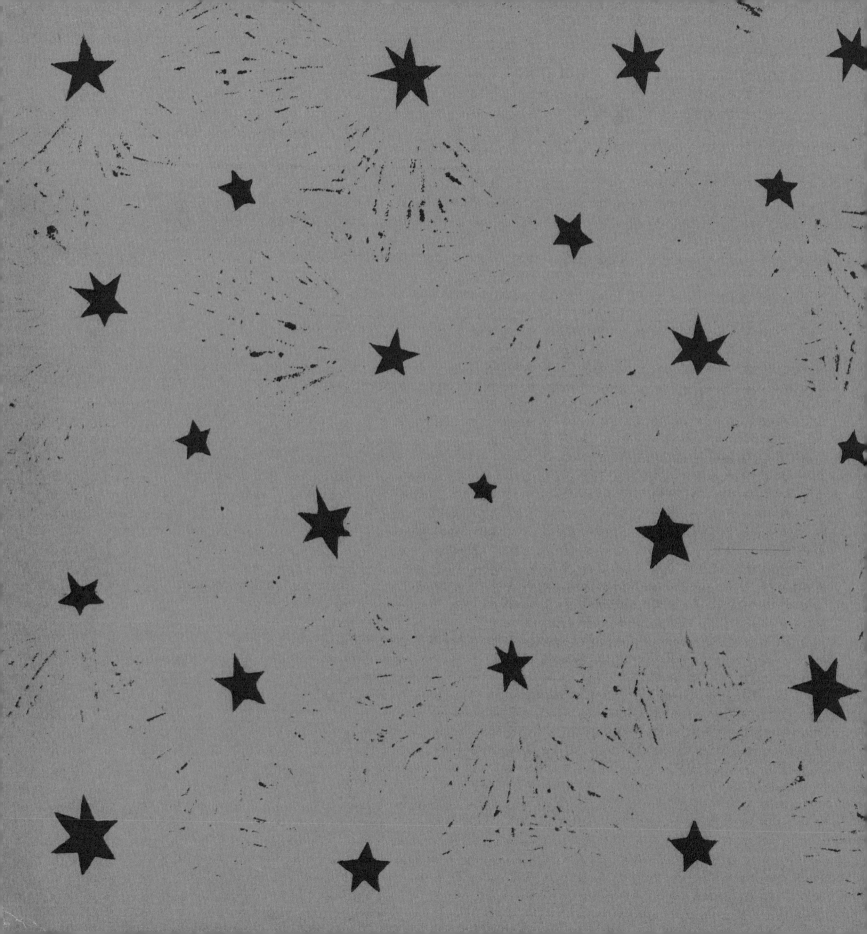

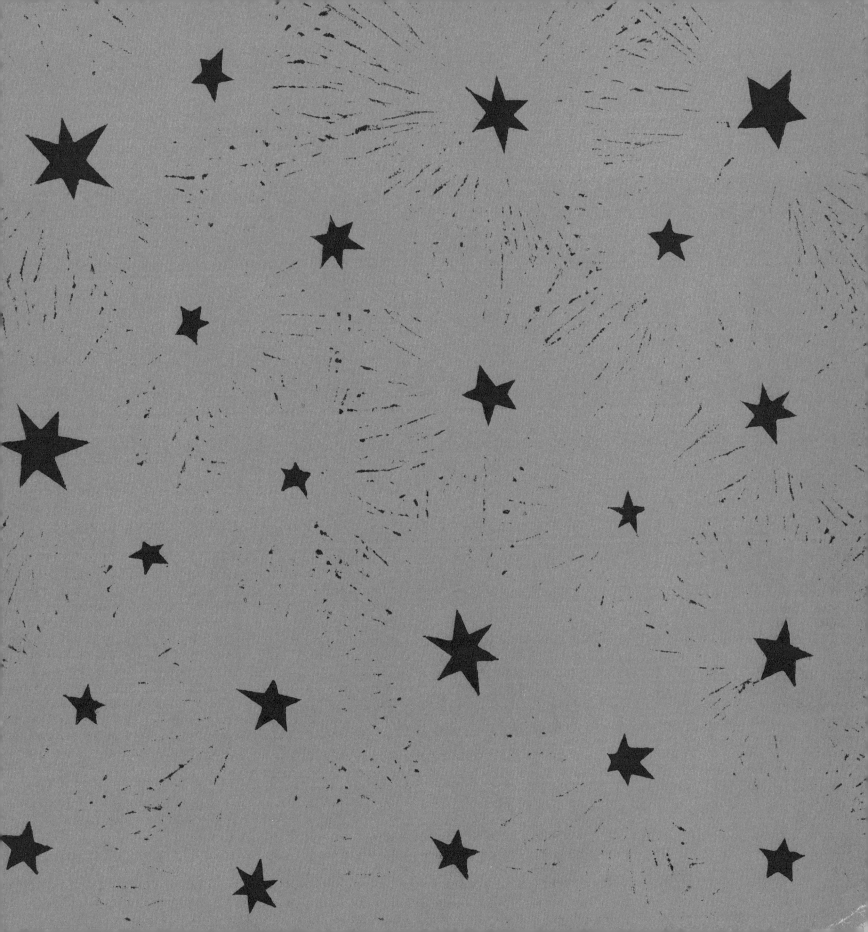

First published 2008 by Macmillan Children's Books
a division of Macmillan Publishers Limited
20 New Wharf Road, London N1 9RR
Basingstoke and Oxford
Associated companies throughout the world
www.panmacmillan.com

ISBN: 978-0-230-70538-8 (hb)
ISBN: 978-0-230-70539-5 (pb)

3 5 7 9 8 6 4 2

A CIP catalogue record for this book is available from the British Library.

Printed in Belgium

The Haunted House

Kazuno Kohara

MACMILLAN CHILDREN'S BOOKS

Once there was a girl who went to live in a big old house at the edge of town. It was a splendid place, but there was one problem.

The house was . . .

...haunted!

But the girl wasn't just a girl.

She was a witch!

She knew how to catch ghosts.

"How lovely," she said.
"I hope there are some more!"

And there were.

She carried on until she had caught

all the ghosts in the house.

Then she went to the kitchen . . .

... and put them all in the washing machine.

When they were clean she hung them out in the garden.

It was fine weather for drying.

After drying, most of the ghosts became nice curtains.

One of them made a good tablecloth.
They were all very useful.

The little witch began to feel very tired
after her hard work.

She knew just what to do with the last two ghosts . . .

And they all lived happily ever after.

In a big old house at
the edge of town there's a
spooky surprise in store . . .

But who's afraid of a few ghosts?
Not this little girl!

MACMILLAN
UK £5.99
CDN $12.99

ISBN 978-0-230-70539-5